SANTA CLAUS
WAS ONCE A KID TOO

By Philip H. Scharper, Jr. and Grace M. Scharper
With Illustrations by Tara J. Hannon

Santa Claus was once a kid too.

Like many other kids, sometimes he did not do everything that his parents wanted him to do.

On a cold day in December, Mother and Father Claus
told Kid Santa to wear his woolen double-breasted red
coat, insulated mittens and white snow pants.

Instead, Kid Santa wore
a spring jacket, an aloha shirt, bermuda
shorts and sandals.

Later, Kid Santa's head felt burning hot, his nose stuffy, his throat scratchy, his stomach rumbly and all of his muscles achy.

Dr. Ursus diagnosed Kid Santa with influenza. "Rest in bed, eat chicken soup, take your medicine and for goodness sake, dress warmly! I'll see you on December 27th."

"Oh no!" Mother Claus said,
"That's two days after Christmas!"

"How will you be able to deliver presents this year?"
Mother Claus asked anxiously.

"Don't worry, I'll ask the Easter Bunny for help. He's used to bringing baskets to kids."

"Fluffy," Kid Santa said, "I'm sick and I won't be able to deliver presents this year. Can you help me?"

The Easter bunny gasped. "You know I'm a spring time animal. I don't like cold weather! And I don't have any winter clothes to wear!"

After eating a bowl of chicken soup and taking his medicine, Kid Santa called the Tooth Fairy.

"Pearly, you know how to deliver gifts to kids when they lose their teeth, right? Can you deliver all the presents on Christmas?"

The Tooth Fairy had the same
disgusted look on her face that she
did whenever she found out that kids
weren't brushing their teeth at least
twice a day.

"Kid Santa," she said with her teeth clenched, "I have never visited every kid in the world on the same night! I would get lost.

Plus chimneys are sooty and I don't want my teeth to turn black."

Then Kid Santa saw Comet's moist, black nose poke through his bedroom window.
"I can help you!" Comet said confidently.

"Won't you get cold?" Kid Santa asked. "Not with your woolen red coat," Comet said.

"But won't you get lost?" Kid Santa asked.

"Not with the help of Dibbles and Nibbles," Comet replied. Dibbles and Nibbles were two of Comet's favorite elf friends.

Dibbles' sense of direction was as good as a homing pigeon. He would make sure that the reindeer didn't get lost.

Nibbles' sense of smell was as good as an elephant.

He could sniff out all the houses with toothsome cookies and clean chimneys.

Dear Santa
Merry Christmas
Love,
Gracie
P.S. Sorry the cookies are bu

On Christmas Eve,
Kid Santa watched as Comet, Dibbles
and Nibbles loaded up the sleigh.

He was relieved to know that, thanks to his friends, millions of
children would not be disappointed on Christmas day.

This was the first and last year that Kid Santa did not go on this magical ride. From that day on, Kid Santa always dressed warmly when the weather got cold-- just as Mother and Father Claus had told him.

17212955R10021

Made in the USA
Middletown, DE
13 January 2015